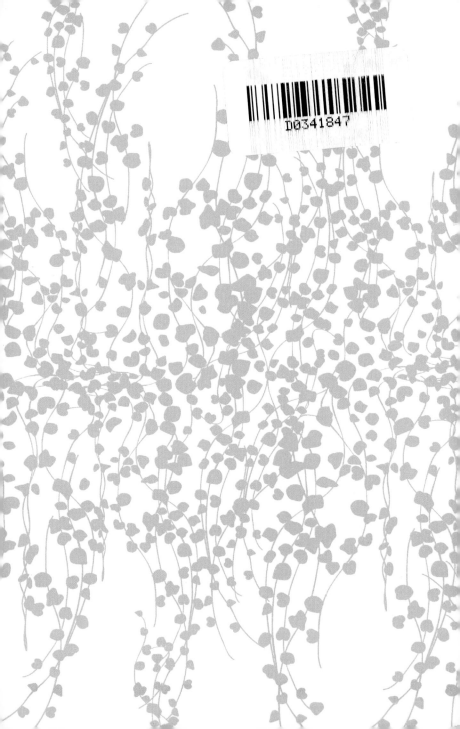

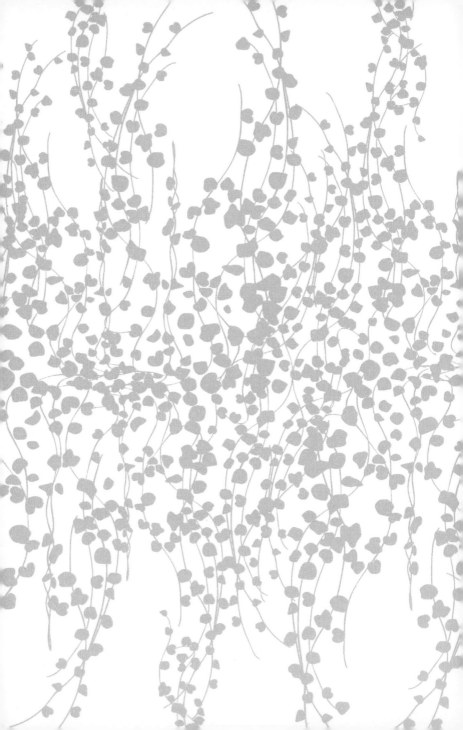

Tiana
The Stolen Jewel

By Calliope Glass
Illustrated by the
Disney Storybook Art Team

DISNEP PRESS
Los Angeles • New York

Printed in China
First Box Set Edition, May 2017
1 3 5 7 9 10 8 6 4 2
FAC-025393-17142
ISBN 978-1-368-00885-3

For more Disney Press fun, visit www.disneybooks.com

Tiana
The Stolen Jewel

"Dreams do
come true in
New Orleans!"
—Tiana

Tiana looked around the kitchen at her new restaurant and smiled. A pot of gumbo bubbled on the stove. Loaves of fresh-baked bread steamed on a cooling rack. A bright pile of carrots sat on the cutting board, ready to be cut up. Amazing smells rose from every corner of the kitchen. The scene made Tiana's heart glow . . . and her nose twitch.

Outside, the first customers were arriving at Tiana's Palace for Sunday dinner. It was the restaurant's busiest night of the week. Tiana wanted to make sure that everyone got a great meal. She bustled around the kitchen, checking on all the dishes.

"Needs lemon juice," she decided, tasting the gumbo. She sliced a lemon in half and squeezed some juice into the pot.

She sampled it again and sighed happily. "There, perfect."

Next Tiana lifted a loaf of bread off the rack. She tapped her finger on its crusty bottom, smiling at the hollow *thunk* it made. It was ready to eat.

Tiana sifted some fine white sugar over the beignets as a finishing touch. Now they were ready, too.

Gazing around the kitchen, Tiana did a final tally. "The gumbo is ready. The soup is done. The bread is baked. We've got hot beignets and cold sweet tea. . . ."

Dinner was nearly ready. All that was left to prepare was the salad and the carrots.

Tiana quickly rinsed some salad greens and set them aside. Then she began chopping the carrots. She hummed a little as she worked. Music was a big part of Tiana's life—especially jazz music. After all, she lived in New Orleans. You couldn't walk down the street here without stumbling across a jazz band playing a tune.

But Tiana's life had more music in it than most, even for New Orleans. Her friend Louis, an alligator, was the best jazz trumpeter around. And her husband, Naveen, played the ukulele with Louis's band at Tiana's Palace.

Naveen wasn't just a musician, of course. He was also a prince . . . and that made Tiana a princess. She still wasn't used to it. "Princess

Tiana!" Tiana laughed as she tossed the chopped carrots into a hot pan. What a strange twist of fate! But that was life. Tiana had learned that no matter how much you planned, you could never guess what was coming.

All her life, Tiana had worked as hard as she could, saving up money to open a restaurant. She'd had it all planned out. But her plan had *not* included being turned into a frog . . . or falling in love with another frog, who was really a human prince! Luckily, Tiana and Naveen had become human again, with the help of Mama Odie, a magic woman who lived in the bayou.

No wonder my plan went astray, Tiana thought. *Nobody* could plan for Mama

Odie. She was just too odd! Tiana shook her head and started humming again. The carrots sizzled in the hot butter as though they were humming along with her.

Suddenly Tiana realized it wasn't just the carrots—another voice had joined hers. She turned around. Prince Naveen had come into the kitchen and was singing along with Tiana.

"Hello, my sweet princess," Naveen said, swooping down for a quick kiss.

Tiana smiled up at him. "You know I'm happy to see you," she said, "but shouldn't you be out there?" Tiana pointed to the dining room, where Louis's band, the Firefly Five, was playing for the guests.

"Louis is playing a solo," Naveen

explained. Tiana smiled again and rolled her eyes. Louis's solos could go on for a while. "So I have plenty of time," Naveen said.

"Then do me a favor," Tiana said. She fished a soft-cooked carrot out of the pan. "Taste this. How is it?"

"Hmm." Naveen chewed thoughtfully. "Well . . ."

"Yes?" Tiana prompted.

"It's just . . ." Naveen trailed off. He frowned.

"What?" Tiana demanded. "More salt? Too much salt? More dill? Pepper? *What?*" She was getting worried.

"No. . . ." Naveen said. His frown became more of a scowl. "It's—what's the word . . . ?" He waved his hands helplessly.

7

"Overcooked?" Tiana guessed. "Not cooked enough? Awful? Disgusting?" Now she was really panicking.

"*Perfect!*" Naveen cried. "That's the word. Perfect!"

Tiana heaved a sigh of relief. She found Naveen's broken English charming . . . most of the time. But Sunday dinners always made her nervous. There was just so much that could go wrong!

"Thank you," she said, kissing his cheek.

"Thank *you*," he said, winking. "I think Louis is finally finishing his solo." Out in the dining room, Tiana could hear Louis playing his heart out.

"Get out there, then," Tiana said. She pushed Naveen playfully. "Shoo!"

"Torn between my two great loves . . ." Naveen said. He put his hand over his heart dramatically. "Music and my princess!"

Tiana blew him a kiss. Then she turned back to her carrots. She gave them one last stir before she turned the flame off. Her life wasn't what she'd planned for . . . it was even better. Her restaurant was a hit. Her best friend, Charlotte, was always there for her. And her husband was a prince—literally.

"Well," Tiana said to herself as she started preparing bowls of salad, "Time for dinner!"

But dinner was not ready to be served after all. As Tiana picked up the first salad bowl, a flamingo flew through the window and landed right in her basket of fresh, hot beignets.

Chapter Two

"My beignets!" Tiana cried. *Now what* would she serve for dessert?

"Oh my goodness gracious, child, I am *so sorry* about that," the flamingo said. He hopped to his feet and shook his feathers out. Powdered sugar flew everywhere. "I'm *never* this clumsy," the flamingo went on, "but I've been flying *ever* so long! I am just plum tuckered out."

Tiana remembered the manners her mama had taught her and said, "Don't you worry about it one second more." She reached out a hand to steady the flamingo, who was wobbling on his long legs. "You look exhausted. Please, sit down. I'll get you some sweet tea."

It was not every day that Tiana had a conversation with a flamingo. She did talk to other animals, though. Ever since she'd been turned into a frog, she could understand animals—and they could understand her. It was the same for Naveen.

"You must be Tiana," the flamingo said. He flopped into a chair.

"That's me," Tiana said. She sat down at the table with the flamingo and poured him a cool glass of iced tea. He dipped his bill in it, drinking thirstily. "I'm Alphonse," he said when he came up for air. "I'm *awfully* pleased to make your acquaintance."

"What brings you to Tiana's Palace?" Tiana asked politely. She tried not to fidget, but she was nervous about the time. It would be rude to get up and start serving dinner in the middle of her conversation with Alphonse, but she didn't want to keep her guests waiting! She hoped whatever he had to say was brief.

"Well, it's a *terribly* long story," Alphonse said. "I do hope you have *lots* of time."

"Um . . ." Tiana said. "I mean . . ."

Just then, the door to the kitchen banged open. It was Tiana's best friend, Charlotte. She dined at the restaurant every Sunday night.

"Tiana, sweetie, what's the holdup?" Charlotte asked. "My second cousin Lucinda is visiting from out of town, and I told her this is the best restaurant in all New Orleans, but we've been waiting for *ages*, and she's getting cranky! Crank*ier*, really. She's a bit of a crank already. Is everything okay back here? All your waiters are, well, waiting for you!"

Then Charlotte saw Alphonse. "Oh, my stars! Why is there a flamingo in your kitchen?" Charlotte paused. Then she whispered, "Is it going into the gumbo?"

"Lottie, thank goodness you're here!" Tiana cried. She'd never been so happy to see her friend in her whole life. "Can you help me out? I really need to get the salad served, but Mr. Alphonse here has just arrived." She pointed at the flamingo. "I think he has something to tell me."

Charlotte rolled her eyes and smiled. "Your life is very strange, *cherie*," she told Tiana. "But that's why I love you! Leave it to me."

Tiana smiled back. Charlotte was the best friend she could ask for. True, she was a bit of a chatterbox, and she got distracted rather easily, but she was loyal to the core.

While Charlotte bustled about putting together dishes for Tiana's customers, Tiana turned back to Alphonse, who began his very long story.

"... and that's when I knew I had found the right place. The neon lights were the final clue. So I flew in the window, and the rest is history! Sorry again about your beignets."

Tiana gaped at him. The flamingo was chattier than Charlotte! He had been talking nonstop for the last forty minutes.

"So, let me get this straight," Tiana said. "Mama Odie sent you because she wants me to visit her."

"Precisely!" Alphonse said. His head bobbed at the end of his long, long neck.

"But why?"

"I've got absolutely no idea! But did I mention it's terribly urgent?"

Tiana stood up and clapped her hands. "All right," she said. "I've got to finish the dinner rush. After we close, we'll tell Naveen and Louis all about it."

* * *

"We're goin' back to the bayou?" Louis exclaimed. He was sitting in the kitchen with Tiana, Naveen, and Alphonse. They were sharing the last of the beignets Tiana had made to replace the ones Alphonse had landed on. The dinner guests had all gone home full and happy, and Tiana's eyelids were starting to droop. Sunday dinner always wore her out.

"Well," Tiana said, "if you're willing. I surely would like the company."

"You bet!" Louis said. "Oh, how I've missed the bayou! The swampy air . . . the greasy water . . . the mosquitoes . . . the snakes . . ."

Naveen shuddered. "You really miss those things?" he asked.

"Well . . . no," Louis admitted. "But there's

no way I'm lettin' Tiana go back there alone. She'll be safer with me."

"Very true," Alphonse said, nodding earnestly. "Nobody wants to tangle with an alligator. All those long, crooked, sharp teeth. And they have *awful* breath. Why, gators are just the absolute worst!"

There was an awkward pause. "Uh, no offense, Louis," Alphonse added.

"None taken," Louis said politely. "I'll watch out for you, too, Alphonse."

Alphonse ruffled his feathers. "I'm much obliged to you, my snaggle-toothed friend," he said, "but I'll be *flying* back to Mama Odie's. There aren't so many hungry things with claws up in the air."

"*I* could go with you," Naveen said.

Tiana reached out and took his hand. "You have to stay," she said. She squeezed his fingers. "I need you to run the restaurant while I'm gone."

"*Me?*" Naveen gulped nervously. "What about Charlotte?"

Tiana shook her head. "Lottie's second cousin Lucinda is visiting. She'll be busy playing hostess."

"Well," Naveen said, "all right. But you will leave me a list, yes? So I don't forget anything."

"Oh yes," Tiana said. "I will *definitely* leave you a list."

Chapter Three

"This is not a *list*, Tiana," Naveen cried. "It is an *encyclopedia*!"

Naveen waved the bundle of pages at Tiana. He had a panicked look on his face.

"It's as short as I could make it," Tiana said apologetically. "Running the restaurant is complicated!"

She picked up her suitcase. Beside her, Louis hefted his trumpet and a picnic basket—his only luggage for the trip.

"Just don't forget to clean the oven," Tiana reminded Naveen.

"I won't—" Naveen began.

"And remember to put fresh candles on all the tables!"

"Yes, Tiana—"

"And today is market day! Make sure you get enough crawfish for the gumbo."

"All right—"

"And don't worry!" Tiana said. She waved good-bye as she and Louis left. "It'll be fine!"

Naveen waved back. He looked worried.

When they were out of earshot, Louis

turned to her. "You really think it'll be fine?"

Tiana nodded brightly. "Of course!"

Louis looked skeptical. *"Really?"*

"No," Tiana sighed. "Not really."

Honestly, Tiana didn't like leaving Naveen alone to run the restaurant. She didn't like having *anyone* but her run the restaurant. But she had no choice. Mama Odie wanted her to visit. And Mama Odie wasn't the sort of person you said no to.

The two friends moved as fast as they could. Tiana wanted to reach Mama Odie's houseboat before nighttime. It wasn't long before they were deep in the swampy heart of the bayou.

"Hey, Tiana!" Louis said. He pointed a finger at a bog. "Remember this spot?"

Tiana squinted. She thought it looked just like every other pond they'd walked by. But then she spotted a familiar-looking hollow tree.

"Yes!" she said. "Louis, isn't this where we first met?"

Tiana and Naveen had been frogs at the time. And they'd been terribly frightened of Louis. But Louis had admired Naveen's musical talent, so instead of eating the frogs, he'd made friends with them. Music was everything to Louis.

"It sure is! This used to be my home," he said. Then he sighed. "I wonder if anyone even noticed that I left."

"Did you have any friends here?" Tiana asked.

Louis brightened up at the question.

"Well," he began, "there was Willie, and Maybelle, and Vincent—"

"Stop right there!" a voice yelled. Three huge, mean-looking alligators were swimming toward Tiana and Louis . . . fast!

"It's Louis!" one of them yelled. *"Don't let him get away!"*

"Freeze!" yelled another one. "Don't you move one inch!" The alligators sped up. Tiana could see sunlight glinting off their sharp teeth. Their tails lashed in the muddy water.

"Uh-oh," Louis said. He grabbed Tiana's hand and the two of them ran for it. They crashed through broken reeds. They got tangled up in tree moss. They slipped on rotting leaves. But when they stopped to catch their breath, they were alone. They had outrun the other alligators.

"Who was that?" Tiana asked, gasping for breath.

"That was Willie, and Maybelle, and Vincent," Louis said glumly.

"I thought they were your friends?" Tiana said.

"I guess not," Louis replied. He looked sad.

"Oh, Louis," Tiana said. "I'm so sorry." She hugged her friend.

Louis shrugged, putting on a brave face.

"Where are we, anyway?" he said, looking around.

"Right where I want you!" a voice called.

It was Mama Odie! Tiana looked up and saw the old woman. She was standing in her house, an old boat stuck in the branches of a huge tree. Poking his long neck out of the window next to Mama Odie, Alphonse waved a feathered wing at Tiana.

"Mama Odie! Hello!" Tiana cried, waving.

"Glad you could make it, child!" Mama Odie called down. "Alphonse here told me you'd be comin' along as fast as you could scramble. And here you are!"

"Scrambling is about right," Tiana said, brushing twigs out of her hair. "We've had a fine time of it!"

"Sounds like you could use a hot meal," Mama Odie said.

"Oh *my*, yes," Louis said. Tiana nodded eagerly.

"How would you like a nice, spicy bowl of gumbo?" Mama Odie asked.

Tiana's stomach rumbled. In all of the confusion with the alligators, she and Louis had completely forgotten to eat lunch! She couldn't wait to sit down and eat something. "That would be wonderful," she said.

"Then come on up here and make us some dinner, child!" Mama Odie yelled. She waved a wooden spoon at Tiana and disappeared into the house.

Tiana smiled and shook her head. Then she started up the stairs. After all, Mama Odie wasn't the kind of person you said no to.

Chapter Four

Tiana tied an apron around her waist. She was tired, but not too tired to cook. In fact, Tiana was *never* too tired to cook. She hummed to herself, just as she always did, while she chopped the celery, peppers, and okra.

Louis was sprawled in an armchair

near the fire. As Tiana sang, he played along softly on his trumpet. Mama Odie tapped her foot in time, while her snake, Juju, bobbed his head sleepily.

Tiana had been making gumbo as long as she could remember. It came naturally to her. And it always reminded her of her father. He'd been the best cook Tiana had ever known. Right now, she could practically hear her father's warm voice. She could almost feel his strong arms around her. Making gumbo was like being with him again. It made her feel loved.

"Look at you go," Mama Odie said. "I never met a girl who loved feedin' people the way you do."

Tiana smiled. "That's why I've got my

restaurant," she said. As she whisked the sauce, she wondered how Naveen was doing. Monday night was usually pretty quiet, but there was still a lot to do! *I just hope he remembers to make the corn bread*, she thought. The idea of Naveen baking corn bread was so strange and funny that Tiana laughed out loud.

Then she began to worry. What if he *burned* the corn bread? What if there was a fire in the kitchen? Tiana stopped stirring the gumbo. Her heartbeat sped up. What if the restaurant burned down? Or, what if the restaurant *didn't* burn down, but the customers hated the food? That would almost be worse!

"Child!" Mama Odie said sharply. Tiana

jumped and came back to herself. Mama Odie scowled at her. "Quit your frettin' and bring me some dinner," she said.

Tiana smiled. Mama Odie was pretty bossy, but she always knew what Tiana needed. And what she had needed just then was a distraction!

Tiana found a small stack of chipped, mismatched bowls on a shelf. She ladled gumbo into five of them and sat down to dinner with Mama Odie, Louis, Alphonse, and Juju. The snake flicked his tail at her in thanks.

For a few minutes, nobody spoke. They just sat together, enjoying the good food and listening to the evening birds singing in the bayou.

Finally, Mama Odie pushed her chair back from the table. Her spoon rattled in her empty bowl.

"Not bad, not bad," she said. "I must say, Tiana, it was mighty kind of you to come all this way to make us dinner."

"But Mama Odie," Tiana said, "why did you really ask me to come visit you?"

"Maybe I just wanted a good bowl of gumbo," Mama Odie said. Her eyes were hidden behind the dark glasses she wore, but Tiana felt sure they'd be twinkling if she could see them.

"Somehow I doubt that," Tiana said. She smiled. "I've had your gumbo, Mama Odie, and it's even better than mine."

"And that's a fact!" Mama Odie said.

She cackled loudly. Then the smile left her wrinkled face. "You're right, Tiana. I had another reason to call you here. I need your help."

Chapter Five

Tiana couldn't believe it. Mama Odie needed *her* help? Mama Odie, the most magical woman in New Orleans, the terror of the bayou, needed the help of a humble cook?

"Of course I'll help you however I can," Tiana said. "But what—"

Tiana's breath caught. Mama Odie was holding up a pearl. It was beautiful—large and shiny and perfectly round.

"Pretty, isn't it?" Mama Odie said. "It's even prettier when it's glowing."

"Glowing?" Louis asked. He looked as confused as Tiana felt.

"This pearl has magic powers," Mama Odie explained. "But it only works when it's with its sister."

"Pearls have sisters?" Tiana said.

"Well, *this* one does," Mama Odie said. "See, way back when, before you were born, I found these two pearls in an enchanted oyster deep down in the bayou. They were like two peas in a pod. They've got big magic, but it only works when they're together.

And just last week, well . . . one of them was stolen."

"*Stolen!*" Louis exclaimed.

"How?" Tiana asked. She couldn't believe someone would be able to steal from Mama Odie. She might be blind, but she still knew about everything going on in the bayou.

"No idea!" Mama Odie said. She threw her arms into the air in frustration. "Whoever it is, she is *sneaky*. And powerful, too. It isn't easy to get in and out of the bayou without me noticing. I asked the pearl where her sister is. All she knows is that the thief has hidden it somewhere in New Orleans."

"That pearl can make conversation?" Louis asked, his eyes growing wide.

"If you know how to listen," Mama Odie said. "She says the thief has hidden her sister on a string of normal pearls."

"So," Tiana said, "someone in New Orleans is wearing a magic pearl . . ."

". . . and nobody's any the wiser," Mama Odie finished. "Hold out your hand, child."

Tiana obediently put her hand out. Mama Odie dropped the pearl into her palm and closed her fingers around it.

"Take this back with you to New Orleans," Mama Odie said. "You can use it to find the other one. When they get close to each other, they'll glow. And watch yourself. You're probably dealing with bad magic here."

Tiana clutched her fingers around the

pearl. It was smooth and slightly warm.

"I'll do my best, Mama Odie," she said.

"That's my girl," Mama Odie said.

"How are you gonna find that pearl, Tiana?" Louis asked as they made their way through the bayou the next morning.

Tiana swatted a mosquito and sighed. "I don't know, Louis," she said. "But as soon as we get home, we'll start working on a plan."

"Home?" said a voice.

"But Louis . . ." said another.

". . . we thought *this* was your home," finished a third voice.

Tiana and Louis whipped around. The

three huge alligators they'd seen before were standing behind them.

"Uh," Louis said. He waved. "Hi?"

Before Tiana could even blink, the three alligators leaped at Louis, who disappeared in a pile of scales and tails.

"Louis!" Tiana screamed.

Chapter Six

Tiana grabbed a broken tree branch off the ground. She hefted it and got ready to start swinging. She was going to save Louis, no matter what.

But as it turned out, she didn't need to.

"We *missed* you!" one of the alligators said. Tiana lowered her club, confused. The alligators weren't attacking Louis—they were *hugging* him.

"And we miss that trumpet of yours," another alligator said. "Since you left, the bayou is just so quiet!"

"Yeah," the third one said. "Now the fireflies won't invite us to their parties. They say there's no point if you're not there to play. It's been so boring here!"

"Sorry we scared you yesterday," the first alligator said sheepishly. "We just missed you so much!"

Louis finally made it to his feet. "Gosh, you guys," he said. He was blushing a deep green, and smiling a big, happy, toothy smile. "I missed you, too!"

"Where'd you go?" the smallest alligator

asked. Tiana guessed this was Maybelle. "Is there more music where you live now?"

Louis told his friends all about New Orleans. He told them about Tiana's Palace, and Naveen, and playing the trumpet late into the night while people danced and danced.

"We want to come visit!" the alligators said.

Louis clapped his hands excitedly. He gave Tiana a pleading look.

"Please, Tiana, can they come with us?" he said.

"Actually," Tiana said thoughtfully, "that's not a bad idea." She had a feeling that three extra alligators might just come in handy in the search for the pearl thief.

Walking through New Orleans with one alligator was hard. Tiana knew this from experience. Getting to Tiana's Palace with *four* alligators was almost impossible. Tiana and the alligators waited at the edge of town until the sun had set. Then they crept back toward the restaurant.

"I'm hungry," Maybelle said. "Does this Palace of yours have anything to eat?"

"Just you wait," Tiana said. "You're about to have the best meal of your life." She loved cooking for alligators—they had such big appetites!

The group turned a corner, and there it was. Tiana's Palace! Tiana breathed a big sigh of relief. Her restaurant hadn't burned down after all.

"We'll go in through the back," Tiana said. "I'll fetch y'all something to eat in the kitchen."

But when they walked into the kitchen, Tiana's heart sank.

A pot of jambalaya was boiling over on the stove. Smoke was pouring out of the oven. And the creamed spinach wasn't creamed yet—in fact, it wasn't even washed!

Naveen was running to and fro, trying to get dinner under control. His hair was a mess, and there was soot on his face. Flour covered his clothing. When he saw Tiana, his face lit up.

"My princess!" Naveen cried. He rushed over and swept Tiana up in a big hug. Now she was covered in flour, too. "You must save me! I have made a terrible disaster!"

Tiana looked around. "I can see that," she said. Naveen hung his head. "Don't worry," Tiana said. "Honestly, I thought it would be worse." She winked at him and got to work.

It didn't take too long to get the kitchen sorted out. The jambalaya was just fine, but the bread was no good. Tiana quickly whipped up some corn bread instead. She set the alligators to work cleaning and chopping the spinach while Naveen made the rice. Before long, dinner was ready!

When all the customers had eaten and gone home, Tiana sat down at the kitchen table with Naveen, Charlotte, and Louis. Louis's friends had gone to bed already. Tiana had tucked them in under the water lilies in the garden fountain.

Tiana told Naveen and Charlotte all about Mama Odie's mission. She reached into her pocket and brought out the pearl.

"Woo-ee!" Charlotte said. Her eyes were

wide. Charlotte loved jewelry more than anyone else Tiana knew. "That's a beauty."

"Someone in New Orleans has the other one right now," Tiana said. "But how on earth are we going to find it?"

Chapter Seven

$\mathcal{T}$hey stayed up late that night, eating beignets and planning.

"How about this," Naveen said. "We buy a hot-air balloon. Then, once we're high over the city, we dangle the magic pearl from it on a long string—"

"No," Tiana said. She was afraid of

heights. There was no way she was getting in a hot-air balloon.

"Why don't we hire another magic woman to find the missing pearl for us?" Charlotte suggested.

"*No,*" Tiana and Naveen said together. They loved Mama Odie, but they'd both had trouble with magic. Tiana didn't want to end up as a frog again—or worse. It was bad enough knowing that the thief had magic powers.

"We could get jobs as jewelry cleaners," Tiana said.

"I am not cut out for cleaning *anything,*" Charlotte said. "Not even jewelry."

"Are pearls magnetic?" Louis asked. "We could get a giant magnet, and—"

"Pearls aren't magnetic," Tiana said. The alligator huffed, and they all fell into silence.

Then Charlotte sat bolt upright.

"I've got it!" she gasped. "We'll throw a party!"

Naveen brightened up. "I love parties!" he said.

"How would a party help us find the pearl?" Tiana asked.

"It's *perfect*," Charlotte said. "We'll plan a gala at Tiana's Palace. The theme will be pearls. The food, the decor—it will all have to do with pearls. Everyone will get dressed up and wear their pearls to the party. That way, all of the pearls in New Orleans will be in Tiana's Palace for one night. You're the hostess, so you can get close to every guest.

You can use the magic pearl to sniff out its missing sister."

Tiana was impressed. That wasn't a bad plan. "But what if the thief doesn't come to the gala?"

"Leave that up to me," Charlotte said. Charlotte was the queen of New Orleans high society. If anyone could make the party a success, she could. "I'll make sure that everyone who's *anyone* comes to our party. Even thieves."

"All right," Tiana said, nodding. "Let's do it. I'll plan the menu first thing tomorrow."

"And I'll plan the music!" Louis said.

"I'll help Louis!" Naveen said.

"And I'll handle the decorations!" Charlotte said happily. "When I'm done with Tiana's Palace, it'll be fit for a princess!"

Naveen kissed Tiana's cheek. "Then it's a good thing we have one to show off!"

Tiana dreamed of pearls that night. The next morning, she was still thinking of pearls.

Naveen waved a hand in front of her face. "Hello, Tiana!" he said playfully. "Can you hear me?"

"Sorry!" Tiana said, jumping. She'd been a million miles away! "I was thinking about the menu for the gala."

"Here," Naveen said. He slid a cup of hot chocolate and a warm beignet across the breakfast table. "Maybe breakfast will help your thinking."

Tiana smiled and sipped happily at the hot chocolate.

"I've been thinking about the music, myself," Naveen said. "Do you think Louis's friends can play any instruments?"

"You want *more* alligators in that band?" Tiana said.

"Just for the Pearl Gala," Naveen said. "I'm thinking . . . tambourines! They're small, white, round—the pearls of the music world!"

"Well," Tiana said, "I'm pretty sure *anyone* can play the tambourine, even an alligator."

"Perfect," Naveen said. He ate his beignet in two bites. "So, what's on the menu?"

"You know, for a prince, you have awful manners," Tiana said. "You really shouldn't talk with your mouth full."

Naveen chewed and swallowed. "Princes don't have to have manners," he pointed out. "That's why it is good to be a prince." He winked at Tiana, and she realized he was teasing her. She rolled her eyes, but she couldn't help smiling. Naveen could always make her smile.

"Well," Tiana said, "I've been thinking about the pearl theme. We'll have tapioca pearls for dessert."

"Naturally," Naveen said.

"And oysters for the appetizer," Tiana went on.

"Perfect!"

"And pearl onions in cream sauce as a side dish."

"Delicious!"

"But what should I make for the main course?" Tiana asked. "I'm stumped."

"Hmm," Naveen said thoughtfully. "Maybe Charlotte will have an idea."

But Charlotte was nowhere to be found.

"Have you seen Charlotte?" Tiana asked Louis. He was polishing his trumpet and chatting with Willie, Maybelle, and Vincent.

"Nope," Louis said. "Sorry, Tiana." Then he turned back to his friends. "Hey, do y'all remember back when we thought that crazy old stork was really Santa Claus?"

The alligators all laughed. Willie slapped his knee, and Vincent softly jangled his tambourine.

Tiana left them to their reunion and went back into the restaurant.

"Naveen, have you seen Charlotte?"

Naveen was sitting at the kitchen table with sheets of music spread out in front of him. He was chewing on a pencil and frowning in concentration. Tiana thought he looked adorable.

"Hmm?" Naveen said absently. "Charlotte?"

"Yes," Tiana said. "She was supposed to meet us here an hour ago. To discuss the decorations, remember?"

"Oh," Naveen said. "Yes, that's odd. Charlotte is usually early."

"I know!" Tiana said. "I hope she's all right."

Just then, Charlotte burst in.

"Tiana!" she cried. "Sweetie, I am so *sorry*."

"It's fine!" Tiana said. She hugged Charlotte. "I was just worried, Lottie. I thought maybe something had happened."

"You had the right idea," Charlotte said. She wiped her forehead with a handkerchief. "My cousin Lucinda has been runnin' me *ragged*. First her room was too hot. So we put fans in the windows. Then it was too *loud*. So we oiled the gears in the fans. But she doesn't like the smell of the oil. I swear, there is no pleasing that woman. All she does is complain!"

Tiana was glad she didn't have any

second cousins visiting. She had enough to deal with already.

Charlotte slumped dramatically into a chair. "And she is so *strange*. She eats sassafras leaves for breakfast! She makes tea out of *catnip*!"

"That *is* strange," Naveen said. "Did you know this about her before she came to visit?"

"No!" Charlotte said, throwing her hands up in the air. "I never met the woman before in my life! I didn't even know I *had* a second cousin. But she's not *all* bad. She gave me these gorgeous earrings!"

Charlotte pointed to her ears. Two rubies dangled from her earlobes, glinting in the light. "*Plus*," Charlotte added, "she gave me a diamond bracelet, an emerald tiara, a string of pearls, an opal ring, and a sapphire pin. I don't know how she got all those jewels, but I am *happy* to take them off her hands."

Tiana whistled.

"At least she has good taste," Naveen said.

"She does at that," Charlotte replied.

She sat up straight and clapped her hands, all business. "*Now.* I have some ideas about the decorations for our gala, and I want to tell you *all* about them . . ."

Chapter Eight

$\mathscr{S}$oon, the night of the Pearl Gala arrived. Charlotte had been talking about the party to anyone who would listen. All of New Orleans knew about it, and Tiana had a feeling that almost everyone in the city was planning on coming.

Tiana's Palace had never looked so

splendid. Charlotte had hung strings of fake pearls from the rafters. White candles glowed on the tables. Iridescent seashells glittered in artful arrangements around the candles. Children from the neighborhood were stationed in the corners of the restaurant, blowing soap bubbles into the air. It was like walking into a royal treasure room filled with pearls.

Tiana was glad she'd taken care with her outfit—she didn't want to be outdone by her restaurant! A simple tiara sat on her head, and she wore a flowing white lace gown trimmed with tiny seed pearls and satin shoes in the lightest shade of ivory.

Around her neck, Tiana wore Mama Odie's magic pearl. It was strung on a simple, elegant silver chain so thin you could barely see it.

Naveen gasped when Tiana walked into the restaurant. He was on the stage, playing with Louis and the Firefly Five in one last rehearsal. He dropped his ukulele and leaped off the stage.

"My princess!" Naveen said. He twirled Tiana into a quick dance across the restaurant floor. Back on the stage, the band kept playing. Louis blew his trumpet, and his alligator friends banged their tambourines for all they were worth.

"How do I look?" Tiana asked. She knew the answer, but it was always nice to hear it.

"You," Naveen said seriously, "are the most beautiful princess in the world." He tilted his head thoughtfully. "In fact," he added, "I do believe you are the most beautiful princess in *all of history*."

"You're not so bad yourself," Tiana said, smiling up at him. Naveen always said just the right thing. "But I have to go—"

"—to the kitchen." Naveen finished for her. "I know. I will see you later." He kissed her and sent her twirling toward the kitchen door. Tiana watched him bound back up onto the stage. She took a deep breath and walked into the kitchen.

Inside, everything was orderly and neat. Tiana loved her tidy kitchen. It was bright and warm, and everything was in its place.

Tiana pulled the bread rolls out of the oven. She had worked hard to make sure they were perfectly round. Their tops were glazed with egg white. They looked like big, pillowy pearls.

The tapioca was chilling in the icebox. The oysters were glistening on trays of crushed ice. Several pans of pearl onions were staying warm on the stove. Soon it would be time to unveil her masterpiece. Tiana had invented a new dish for the Pearl Gala: Chicken Pot Pearl. It was like chicken pot pie, but the crust was a perfect sphere of puff pastry. Each beautiful little pie looked like a shining, golden pearl.

Tiana smiled happily. Who knew that catching a thief could be so much fun?

Tiana watched as her guests streamed into

the restaurant. All of New Orleans high society had come. Everyone was dressed to the nines, of course, and all the women were wearing pearls—pearl earrings, pearl necklaces, pearl bracelets. Some even had pearls sewn to their dresses, like Tiana.

Tiana kept an eye on things from the kitchen. The waiters, dressed in white tailcoats, brought out the oysters first. Then they served the main course. Tiana smiled as she heard gasps rise up from all over the room. The Chicken Pot Pearls were a hit!

Finally, the guests were ready for dessert. It was time for Tiana to make her move. She waited until everyone had been served dessert. Then she began making her rounds as hostess. She walked from table to table, shaking people's hands and thanking them for coming. She bent near everyone she greeted, looking for a glowing pearl. Tiana visited table after table, but the missing pearl didn't appear.

Finally, there was only one table left. Tiana's heart sank. It was Charlotte's table. Obviously the pearl wouldn't be there. It looked like the gala was a bust. They'd have to come up with a new plan.

Charlotte and her father were with a scowling, wild-haired older woman. Tiana figured she must be Charlotte's strange second cousin, Lucinda.

Charlotte raised her eyebrows at Tiana, as if to say, *Well? Did you find the pearl?*

Tiana shook her head subtly. Charlotte's face fell. Tiana was feeling pretty gloomy herself. But she put on a brave face. She still had to be a good hostess.

"Welcome to Tiana's Palace," Tiana said. "I'm so glad you could—"

She stopped suddenly. Charlotte was wearing an elegant string of pearls. And the

pearl in the very center of the string was glowing.

Tiana had found Mama Odie's missing pearl . . . around Charlotte's neck!

Chapter Nine

"Tiana . . ." Charlotte said. She was staring at Tiana's necklace.

"Lottie . . ." Tiana said. She was staring at Charlotte's necklace.

"Your pearl! It's glowing!" both of the friends said at once.

Charlotte looked down at her necklace.

"I don't understand," she said. "Why is *my* necklace glowing? Why, I only just got these pearls! They were a gift from . . ."

CRASH! Lucinda overturned her chair. She snatched the pearls from Charlotte's neck, hiked up her skirt, and ran for the door. Everyone in the restaurant turned around and stared. Even the band stopped playing.

". . . Lucinda!" Charlotte finished. "Why, I—Tiana, *she's the thief!* And she's getting away!"

Tiana had planned for this. She put two fingers to her mouth and whistled as loudly as she could. At her signal, Willie, Maybelle, and Vincent dropped their tambourines and leaped off the stage. In a flash, they had Lucinda pinned to the ground.

"*Ugh!*" Lucinda yelled. "Alligators! I hate them."

"She also hates crying babies, muggy weather, loud music, horses, people who sniffle, overcooked pasta, itchy sweaters, and waiters who are just a little bit too friendly," Charlotte told Tiana. They walked over toward where Lucinda was lying on the floor. Maybelle was sitting on her.

"Basically, she never stops complaining," Charlotte said. "I have to say, it doesn't amaze me to learn she's the thief."

"Willie, Vincent, please help Miss Lucinda up," Tiana said. "Take her into the kitchen. I'd like my guests to enjoy the rest of their night in peace."

She watched the alligators drag Lucinda

toward the back of the restaurant. "And don't let her escape!" Tiana called after them.

Tiana apologized to her guests, and the band struck up a cheery tune. As everyone returned to their desserts, Tiana went into the kitchen.

Lucinda was sitting at the kitchen table, sulking. She was still clutching the string of pearls. The alligators were grouped around her, showing their big, pointy teeth. Charlotte glared at Lucinda.

"Are you actually my second cousin?" she demanded.

"Yes," Lucinda said sourly.

"Then why haven't I ever met you?" Charlotte demanded.

"I hate New Orleans!" Lucinda said. "The food is weird, and it's crowded, and there's all of this *jazz music* everywhere."

Maybelle gasped, shocked. "Jazz is wonderful!" she said.

"What would you know?" Lucinda

said. "You're an alligator. Everyone knows alligators have tin ears."

Maybelle growled and bared her teeth.

Tiana decided to step in before things got ugly. "Lucinda," she said.

Lucinda looked over at her, and Tiana held out her hand, palm up. Charlotte's cousin sighed and handed over the pearls.

"Curses," she said, scowling. "Foiled again."

"Why did you give the magic pearl to Lottie?" Tiana asked.

"To hide it," Lucinda said. "I was going to take it with me when I left town tomorrow."

"Well, I never!" Charlotte said. "Were you going to let me keep the *other* jewelry you 'gave' to me?"

"No," Lucinda said. Charlotte looked disappointed. "Well, maybe those ruby earrings," Lucinda said. "They're pretty tacky."

"I love those earrings!" Charlotte said, excited. "They're not tacky at all!"

Lucinda just raised an eyebrow.

"Why did you steal Mama Odie's magic pearl?" Tiana asked.

"To annoy her!" Lucinda said. "The way she annoys me. We've been getting on each other's nerves since before either of you were born. She broke my favorite herb bowl, and I put a polka-dot curse on her. Then she turned my house upside down, so I put her boat in a tree."

"*That's* how it got up there?" Tiana asked.

She'd always wondered.

Lucinda looked proud. "That was me! But then she turned all of my socks into newts a few years back. I've been planning my revenge ever since. Not bad, eh? I took her fancy magic pearl!"

Chapter Ten

$\mathcal{L}$ucinda left town the next morning.

"Have a good trip home," Tiana said.

"I can't wait to get out of here," Lucinda replied. "I hate how this town smells." She stomped down the street.

"And *stay* out," Charlotte muttered as Lucinda disappeared around a corner.

"Charlotte," Tiana said gently. "Don't be rude. She's still your cousin. And she gave you those earrings, after all."

"I suppose," Charlotte said. "But that doesn't make her any less awful."

Tiana brushed her hands on her apron briskly. "Well," she said. "That's that. Shall we have breakfast?"

"Oh, yes!" Charlotte said. She looked excited. "And I know just the place. It's this lovely restaurant that has the *best* beignets."

"Really?" Tiana said. She was a little worried. Charlotte always said *her* beignets were the best. Was there new competition? Or had her skills been slipping? "What restaurant is it?"

"A little old place called Tiana's Palace!"

Charlotte said with a grin. She put her arm through Tiana's, and the two friends went to get breakfast.

⁂

"When do you want to return the pearls to Mama Odie?" Charlotte asked.

Tiana took a bite of beignet and chewed thoughtfully. They were eating breakfast with Louis and Naveen. Outside, Louis's friends were playing in the fountain. Tiana could hear them giggling.

Before Tiana could reply, Louis piped up.

"Tonight! This afternoon! Right now!" Louis said. "She's going to be so happy to see them!"

Tiana shrugged. "Sure," she said. "Why

not? I can close Tiana's Palace for one day."

"You do not want me to stay here and run the restaurant this time?" Naveen asked. He looked relieved.

"Well, my prince," Tiana said, "I have a feeling there's going to be a party in the bayou tonight."

"I love parties!" Naveen said.

"Exactly," Tiana replied. She kissed him on the cheek. "And it wouldn't be a party without you."

Tiana hurried back to the fountain in the garden. "Willie, Maybelle, Vincent!" she called.

"Yes, Tiana?" they said in unison. Tiana giggled. They were like an alligator chorus!

"We're going back to the bayou, y'all!"

she called. "Come on! What are we waiting for?"

<hr>

Tiana felt like she was leading a little parade through the bayou.

She walked hand-in-hand with Naveen. Behind them, Charlotte chattered to Louis. And behind *them*, Willie, Maybelle, and Vincent trotted along single file. A cloud of fireflies brought up the rear. Tiana knew the fireflies never missed a good party, so she had made sure to invite them along.

"Well, aren't you all just adorable!"

Tiana looked up. "Hi, Alphonse!" she said. The flamingo was flying above them, his big wings flapping slowly.

"Mind if I join you?" he asked. "Mama Odie knows you're comin'. She sent me to make sure y'all don't get lost."

When they got to the house, Mama Odie was waiting for them. She leaned against the trunk of the tree.

"I hear you got my pearl back!" she said. Tiana reached into her pocket and pulled out the sister pearls. She'd wrapped them up in a bit of silk. When Mama Odie unwrapped them, they were glowing softly. It was almost as though they were happy to be together, Tiana thought.

Mama Odie sighed happily. She slipped the pearls into her pocket and hugged Tiana. "Thank you, child," she said. "You've done me a great favor."

Tiana hugged her back. "I was happy to do it," she said. Then she paused. A wonderful smell was winding its way down from Mama Odie's boat.

Tiana's nose twitched. "I know that smell," she said. "Grilled catfish!"

"Of course! Is this a party or ain't it?" Mama Odie asked. She grinned.

"It's sure a party *now*," Louis said. "Boy, I love catfish."

"So do we!" Willie, Maybelle, and Vincent said.

"Then come on up," Mama Odie said. "And dig in!"

When they climbed into the boat, Tiana said, "You know, it was Lucinda who took your pearls."

Mama Odie shook her head crossly. "I thought it might have been," she said. "That woman gets on my nerves!"

"She told me she's the one who put your houseboat in a tree," Tiana said.

"That's true enough," Mama Odie said. "But the joke's on her. I like it better up here!"

Tiana laughed. She watched Louis and his friends dig in. There was catfish, grilled okra, potato salad, and dirty rice. "Say, Mama Odie," Tiana said. "I'd love a glass of sweet tea. Do you have any?"

"Yes, child," Mama Odie said. "Because you're makin' a big batch for all of us. Get to work!"

Tiana grinned and got to work.

In no time, the party was in full swing. The friends ate, sang, and danced, their music echoing through the sweet night air. Tiana looked up at the starry sky as she spun in Naveen's arms. It was good to be back in the bayou!